KT-143-834

Mindful Monkey, Happy Panda

Wisdom Publications
199 Elm Street
Somerville, MA 02144

Text © 2011 Lauren Alderfer
Illustrations © 2011 Kerry Lee MacLean

No part of this book may be reproduced in any form or by any means, electronic
or mechanical, including photography, recording, or by any information technology
now known or later developed, without permission in writing from the publisher.

Library of Congress Cataloging-in-Publication Data

Alderfer, Lauren, 1955–
  Mindful Monkey, Happy Panda / story by Lauren Alderfer ; illustrations by
Kerry Lee MacLean.
    p. cm.
  Summary: Monkey asks Panda what he does to seem so happy and peaceful
all the time, and Panda replies that he brings his attention to whatever he is doing
at a given time, whether eating, walking, or resting.
  ISBN 0-86171-683-3 (hardcover : alk. paper)
[1. Meditation—Fiction. 2. Buddhism—Customs and practices—Fiction.
3. Monkeys—Fiction. 4. Pandas—Fiction.] I. MacLean, Kerry Lee, ill. II. Title.
  PZ7.A36135Min 2011
  [E]—dc22
                                                                    2011007531

19 18 17 16 15
8 7 6 5

          ISBN 978-0-86171-683-8, eBook ISBN 978-0-86171-850-4

Cover and interior design by Gopa & Ted2, Inc. Set in Cantoria Semibold 20/28.
Edited and developed by Josh Bartok.

Wisdom Publications' books are printed on acid-free paper and meet
the guidelines for permanence and durability of the Production Guidelines
for Book Longevity of the Council on Library Resources.

Printed in the United States of America.

Books by LAUREN ALDERFER include *Tibetan Proverbs: Children's Voices from
the Homeland*; *How Yak Got His Long Hair*; and *Nine and a Half Fingers*.

Books by KERRY LEE MACLEAN include *Moody Cow Meditates*; *Peaceful Piggy
Meditation*; and *Moody Cow Learns Loving-Kindness* (2012).

MINDFUL MONKEY, HAPPY PANDA

Story by **Lauren Alderfer**   Illustrations by **Kerry Lee MacLean**

WISDOM PUBLICATIONS • BOSTON
www.wisdompubs.org

One late afternoon, as Monkey was walking home
from a long day at school, Monkey came across
Panda, sitting serenely in a thicket of bamboo.

"You always seem so happy and peaceful,"
said Monkey.

"Yes, you could say that,"
said Happy Panda, with a little smile.

"What do you do
to be so happy
and peaceful?"

"I walk,
I work,
I read,
I eat,
I play,
and I rest."

"I walk,
   I work,
   I read,
   I eat,
   I play, and
   I rest, too,
   but I am not
   so happy,"
   said Monkey.

"That seems true,"
   said Happy Panda
   as he looked at Monkey.
"So, Monkey, what do
   you think about when
   you do those things?"

"**Well…**" said Monkey.

"When I walk, I also think about doing chores.

"When I do chores, I also think about reading.

"When I read,
I also
think about
eating.

"When I eat,

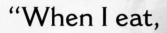

I also think
about playing.

Throw!

"When I play, I also think about resting.

"When I rest,

I also think about walking."

"Ah…" said Happy Panda.

"Your monkey mind

jumps

from one thing

to another,

always to somewhere other than here,
to something other than what you're doing right now."

"**Well, of course it does!**" said Monkey. "Isn't that what everyone's mind does?"

"Well…," said Happy Panda.

"When I walk, I am just walking.

"When I work,

I am just working.

"When I read, I am just reading.

"When I eat, I am just eating.

"When I play, I am just playing.

"And when I rest,

I am just resting.

"True happiness," said Happy Panda gently,
"comes from bringing all your attention to whatever
you are doing right now. There is no need to think
about what happened yesterday. Yesterday's gone,
over, done. And there's no need to worry about tomorrow.
Tomorrow isn't here. But today is all around us.
Bringing your mind back to this moment, right here,
over and over and over again, is called **mindfulness**."

"Oh, I get it!" said Monkey.
"**Mind-full**, like your **mind** is **full** of the present,
full of right now. That's definitely how I want to be!"

And at that very moment,
Monkey started to practice mindfulness.

How about you?